TRANSFORMERS: REVENGE OF THE FALLEN
ISSUE NUMBER FOUR (OF FOUR)

WRITTEN BY: **SIMON FURMAN**

PENCILS BY: **JON DAVIS-HUNT**

COLORS BY: **KRIS CARTER**

LETTERS BY: **CHRIS MOWRY**

EDITS BY: **DENTON J. TIPTON**

ADAPTED FROM THE SCREENPLAY BY: **ROBERTO ORCI, ALEX KURTZMAN, AND EHREN KRUGER**

Special thanks to Hasbro's Aaron Archer, Michael Kelly, Amie Lozanzki, Va Roca, Ed Lane, Michael Provost, Erin Hillman, Samantha Lomow, and Michael Verecchia for their invaluable assistance.

To discuss this issue of *Transformers*, join the IDW Insiders, or to check out exclusive Web offers, check out our site:

   Licensed by:

VISIT US AT
www.abdopublishing.com

Reinforced library bound edition published in 2010 by Spotlight, a division of the ABDO Group, 8000 West 78th Street, Edina, Minnesota 55439. Published by agreement with IDW Publishing. www.idwpublishing.com

Printed in the United States of America, Melrose Park, Illinois.
102009
012010
 PRINTED ON RECYCLED PAPER

Library of Congress Cataloging-in-Publication Data

Furman, Simon.
 Transformers : revenge of the fallen / written by Simon Furman ; pencils by Jon Davis-Hunt colors by Kris Carter and Josh Perez ; letters by Chris Mowry ; adapted from the screenplay by Roberto Orci, Alex Kurtzman, and Ehren Kruger.
  v. cm.
 ISBN 978-1-59961-726-8 (vol. 1) -- ISBN 978-1-59961-727-5 (vol. 2)
 ISBN 978-1-59961-728-2 (vol. 3) -- ISBN 978-1-59961-729-9 (vol. 4)
 1. Graphic novels. I. Davis-Hunt, Jon. II. Orci, Roberto. III. Kurtzman, Alex. IV. Kruger, Ehren, 1972- V. Transformers, revenge of the fallen (Motion picture) VI. Title.
PZ7.7.F87Tr 2010
741.5'973--dc22

                              2009037024

All Spotlight books have reinforced library bindings and are manufactured in the United States of America.

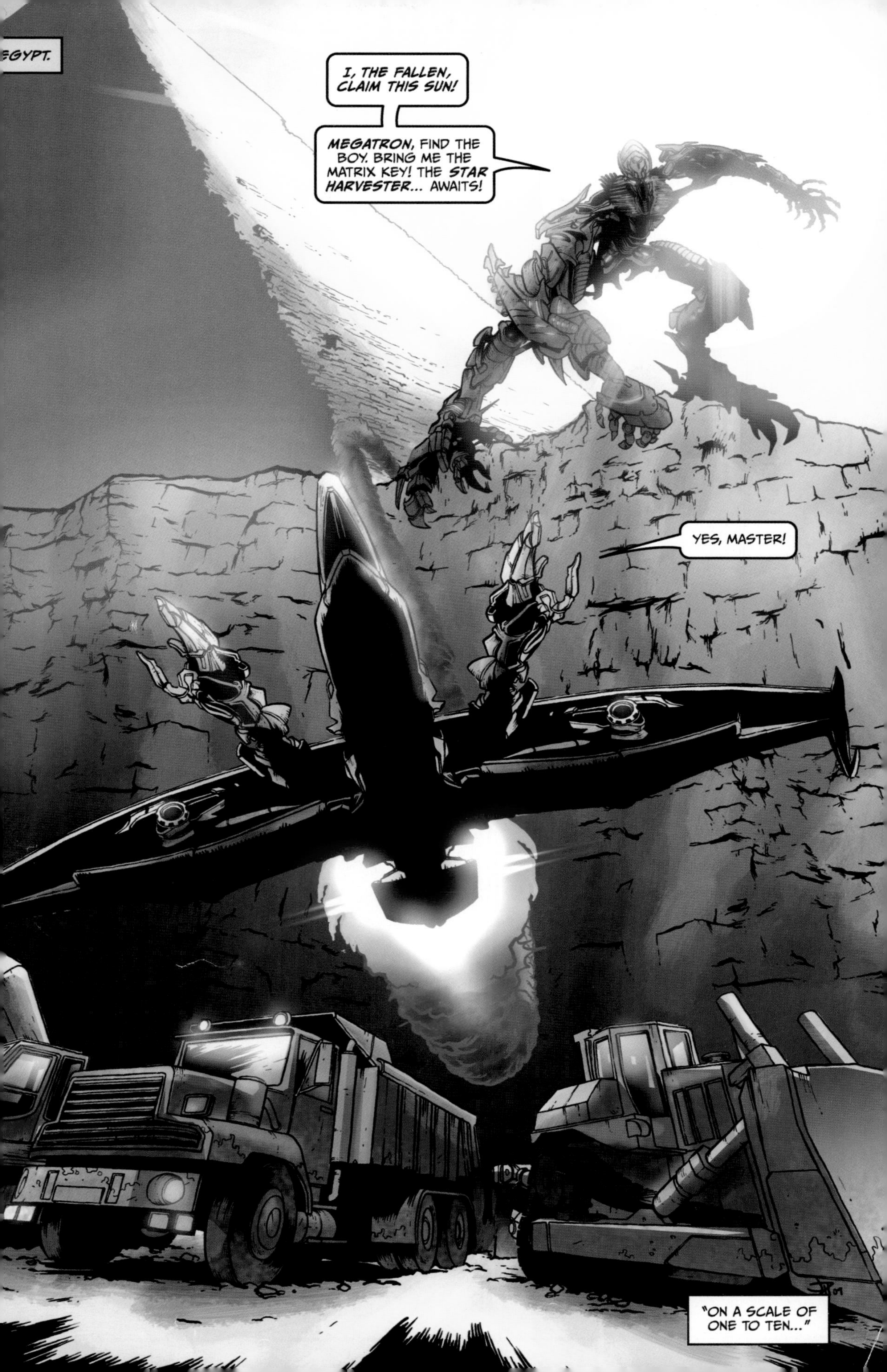
EGYPT.
I, THE FALLEN, CLAIM THIS SUN!
MEGATRON, FIND THE BOY. BRING ME THE MATRIX KEY! THE STAR HARVESTER... AWAITS!
YES, MASTER!
"ON A SCALE OF ONE TO TEN..."

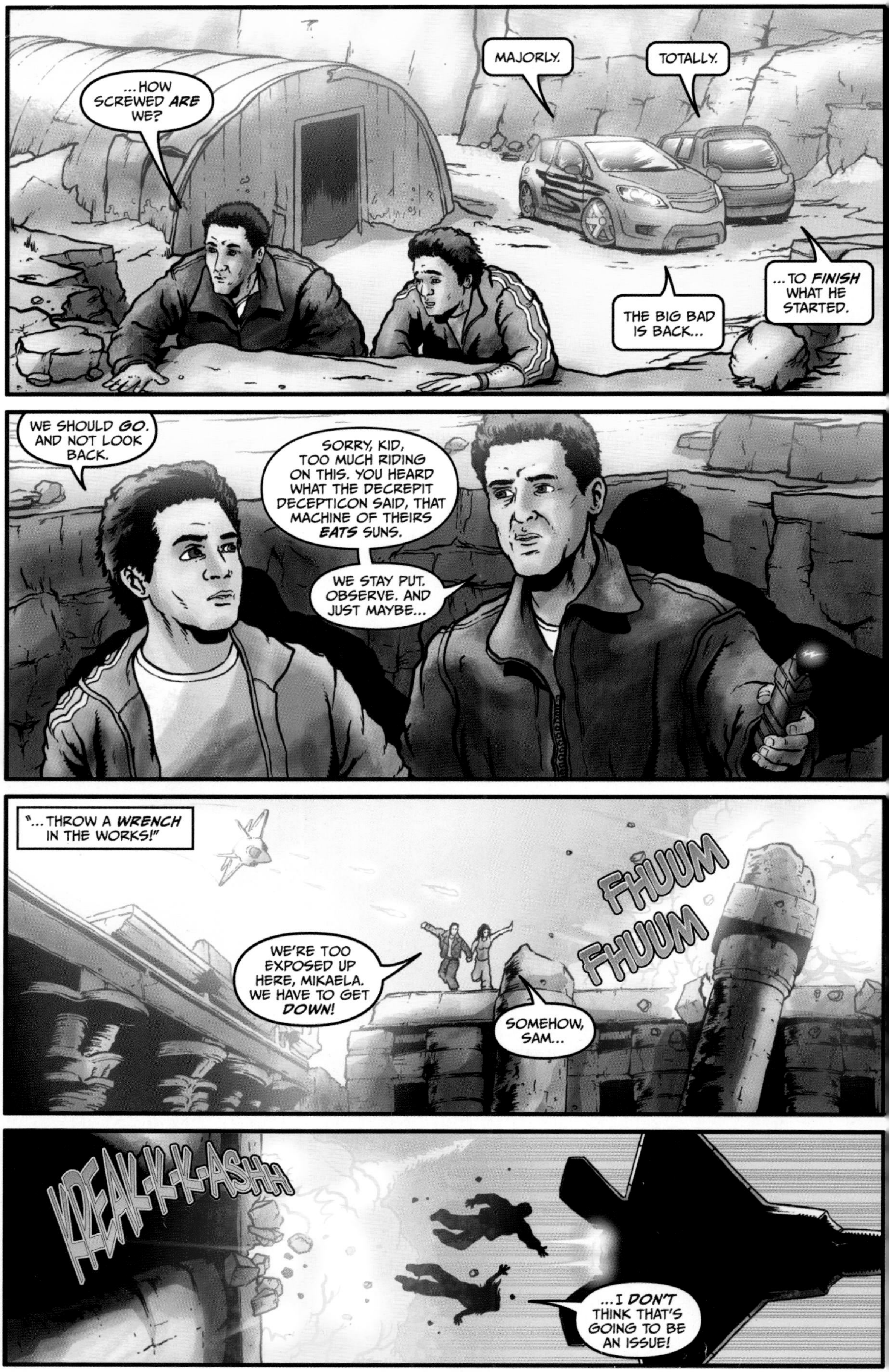
...HOW SCREWED ARE WE?
MAJORLY.
TOTALLY.
THE BIG BAD IS BACK...
...TO FINISH WHAT HE STARTED.
WE SHOULD GO. AND NOT LOOK BACK.
SORRY, KID, TOO MUCH RIDING ON THIS. YOU HEARD WHAT THE DECREPIT DECEPTICON SAID, THAT MACHINE OF THEIRS EATS SUNS.
WE STAY PUT. OBSERVE. AND JUST MAYBE...
"...THROW A WRENCH IN THE WORKS!"
FHUUM
FHUUM
WE'RE TOO EXPOSED UP HERE, MIKAELA. WE HAVE TO GET DOWN!
SOMEHOW, SAM...
KREAK-K-K-ASHH
...I DON'T THINK THAT'S GOING TO BE AN ISSUE!

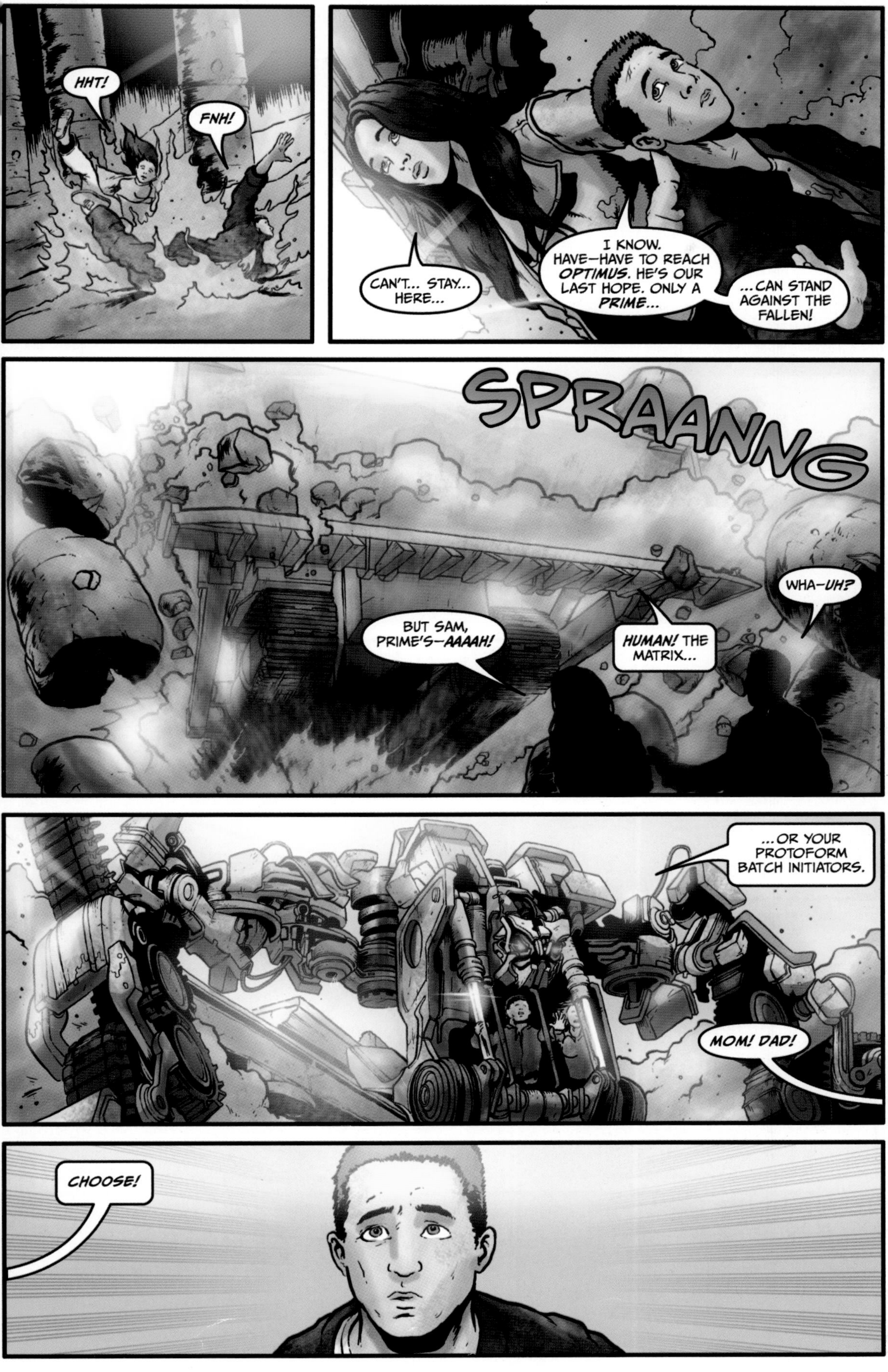
HHT!
FNH!
CAN'T... STAY... HERE...
I KNOW. HAVE—HAVE TO REACH OPTIMUS. HE'S OUR LAST HOPE. ONLY A PRIME...
...CAN STAND AGAINST THE FALLEN!
SPRAANNG
BUT SAM, PRIME'S—AAAAH!
HUMAN! THE MATRIX...
WHA—UH?
...OR YOUR PROTOFORM BATCH INITIATORS.
MOM! DAD!
CHOOSE!

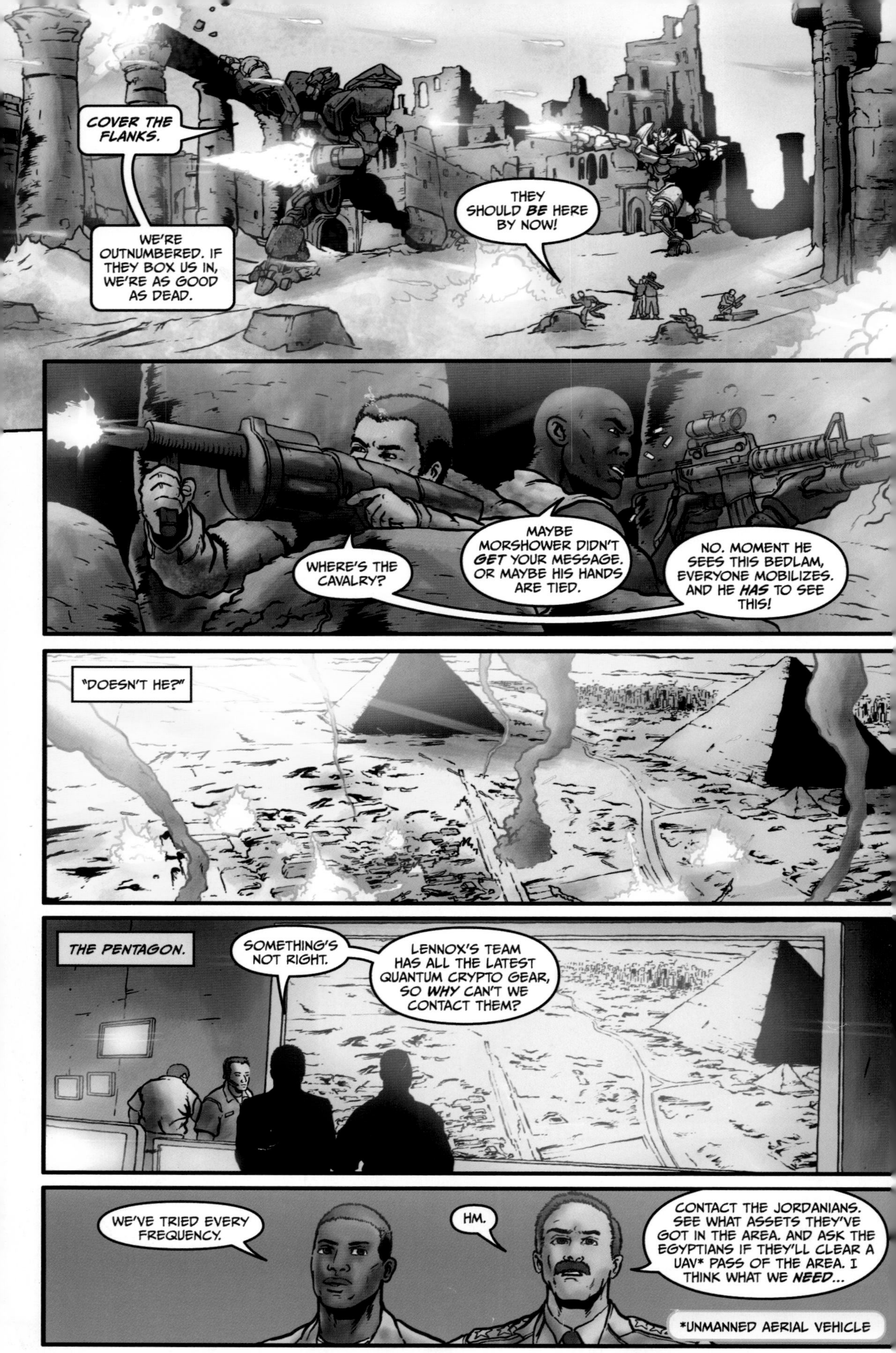
COVER THE FLANKS.
WE'RE OUTNUMBERED. IF THEY BOX US IN, WE'RE AS GOOD AS DEAD.
THEY SHOULD BE HERE BY NOW!
WHERE'S THE CAVALRY?
MAYBE MORSHOWER DIDN'T GET YOUR MESSAGE. OR MAYBE HIS HANDS ARE TIED.
NO. MOMENT HE SEES THIS BEDLAM, EVERYONE MOBILIZES. AND HE HAS TO SEE THIS!
"DOESN'T HE?"
THE PENTAGON.
SOMETHING'S NOT RIGHT.
LENNOX'S TEAM HAS ALL THE LATEST QUANTUM CRYPTO GEAR, SO WHY CAN'T WE CONTACT THEM?
WE'VE TRIED EVERY FREQUENCY.
HM.
CONTACT THE JORDANIANS. SEE WHAT ASSETS THEY'VE GOT IN THE AREA. AND ASK THE EGYPTIANS IF THEY'LL CLEAR A UAV* PASS OF THE AREA. I THINK WHAT WE NEED...
*UNMANNED AERIAL VEHICLE

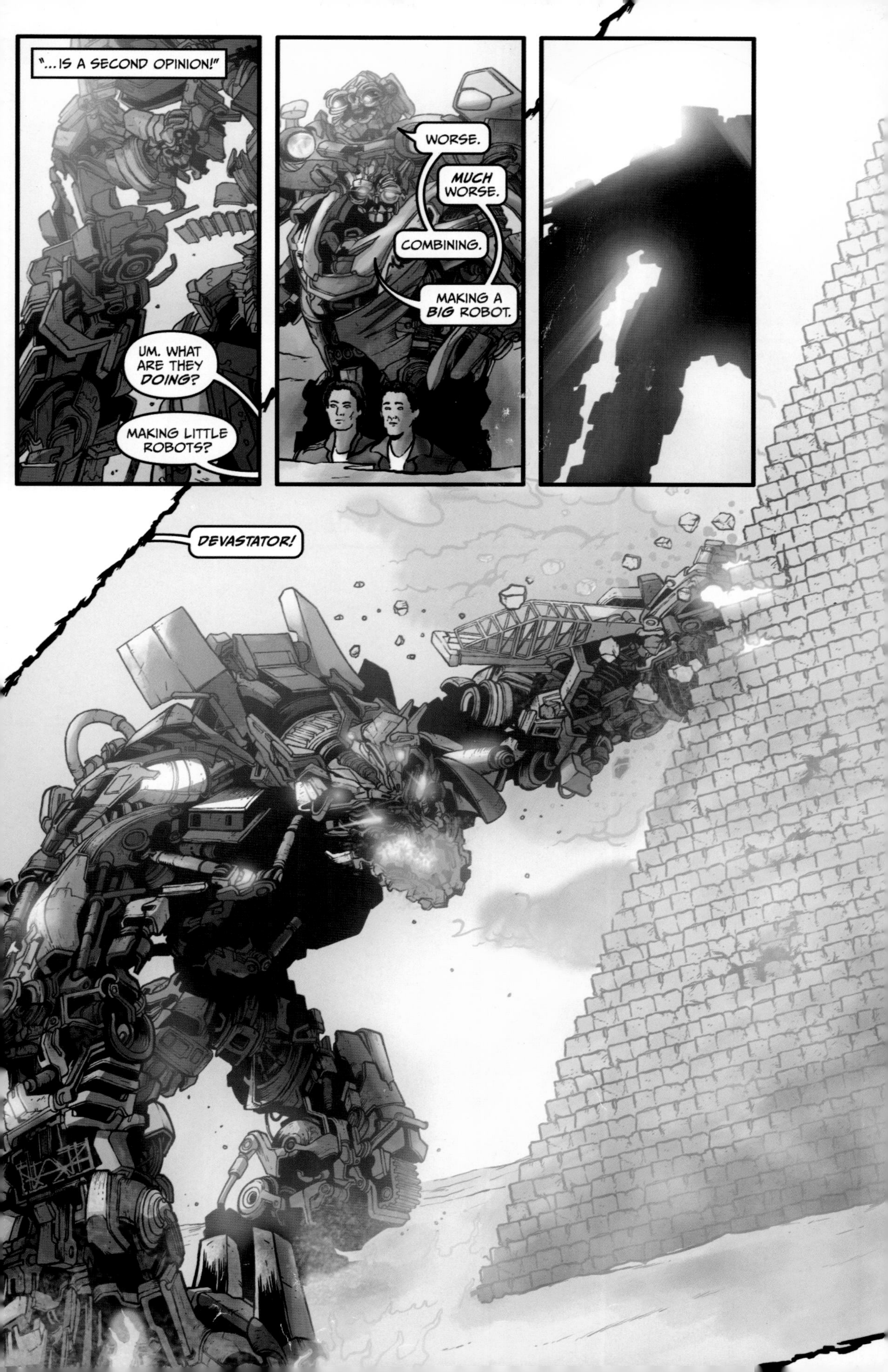
"...IS A SECOND OPINION!"
UM. WHAT ARE THEY DOING?
MAKING LITTLE ROBOTS?
WORSE.
MUCH WORSE.
COMBINING.
MAKING A BIG ROBOT.
DEVASTATOR!

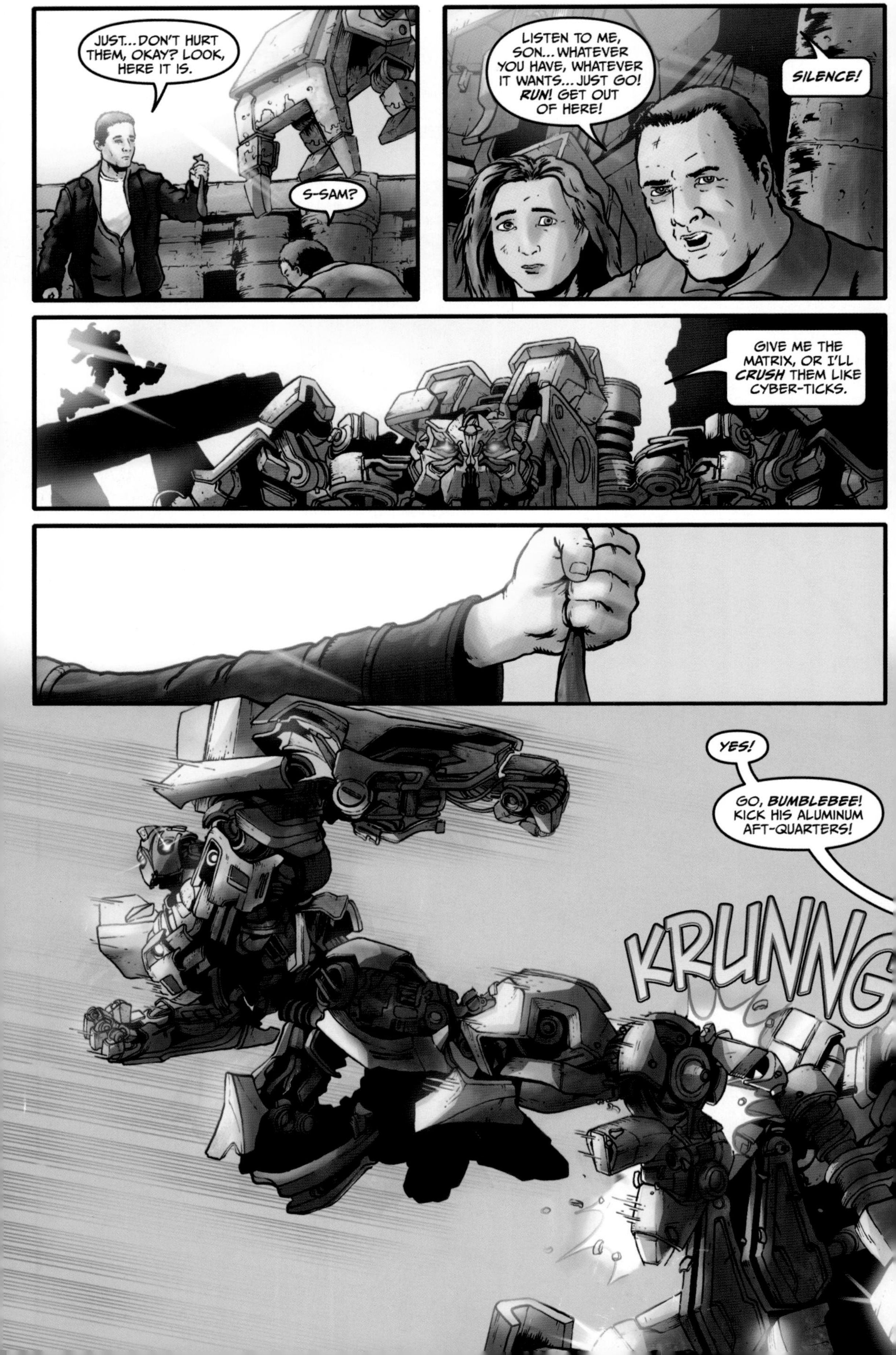
JUST...DON'T HURT THEM, OKAY? LOOK, HERE IT IS.
S-SAM?
LISTEN TO ME, SON...WHATEVER YOU HAVE, WHATEVER IT WANTS...JUST GO! RUN! GET OUT OF HERE!
SILENCE!
GIVE ME THE MATRIX, OR I'LL CRUSH THEM LIKE CYBER-TICKS.
YES!
GO, BUMBLEBEE! KICK HIS ALUMINUM AFT-QUARTERS!
KRUNNG

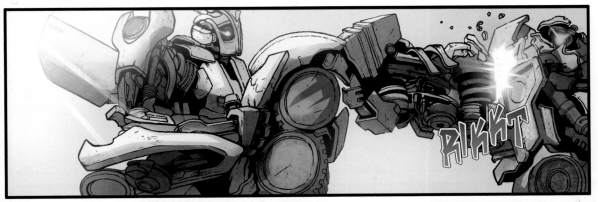

RIKKT

ZTTIK

RUUNNK

SAM, OH SAMMY, THANK GOD.

YOU GO. 'BEE, KEEP THEM SAFE.

WE *HAVE* TO GET OUT OF HERE! C'MON.

WHAT? BUT—

I *HAVE* TO DO THIS, DAD. I HAVE TO SEE THIS THROUGH. JUST...

"...LET ME *GO*."

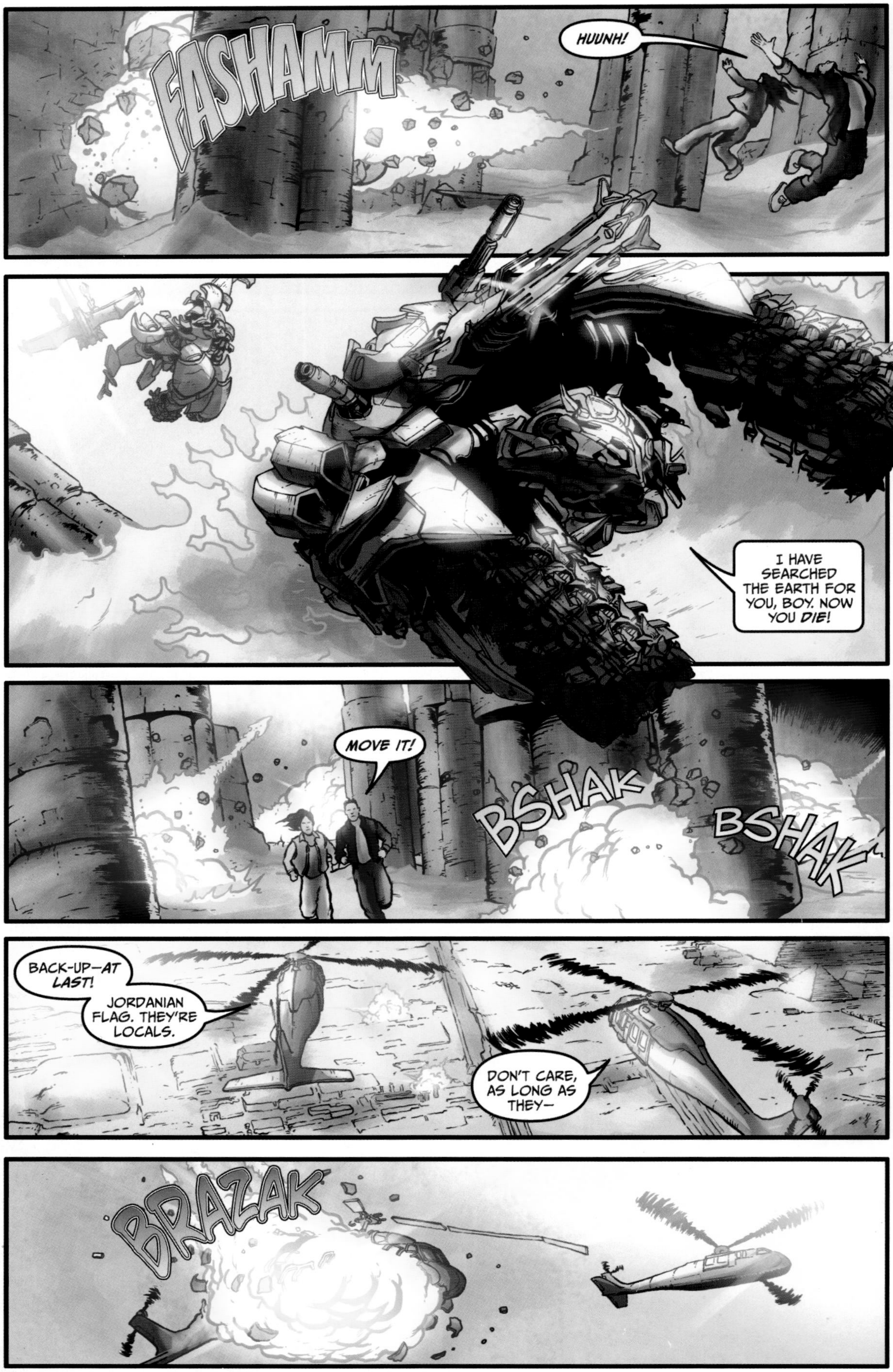
FASHAMM
HUUNH!
I HAVE SEARCHED THE EARTH FOR YOU, BOY. NOW YOU DIE!
MOVE IT!
BSHAK
BSHAK
BACK-UP—AT LAST!
JORDANIAN FLAG. THEY'RE LOCALS.
DON'T CARE, AS LONG AS THEY—
BRAZAK

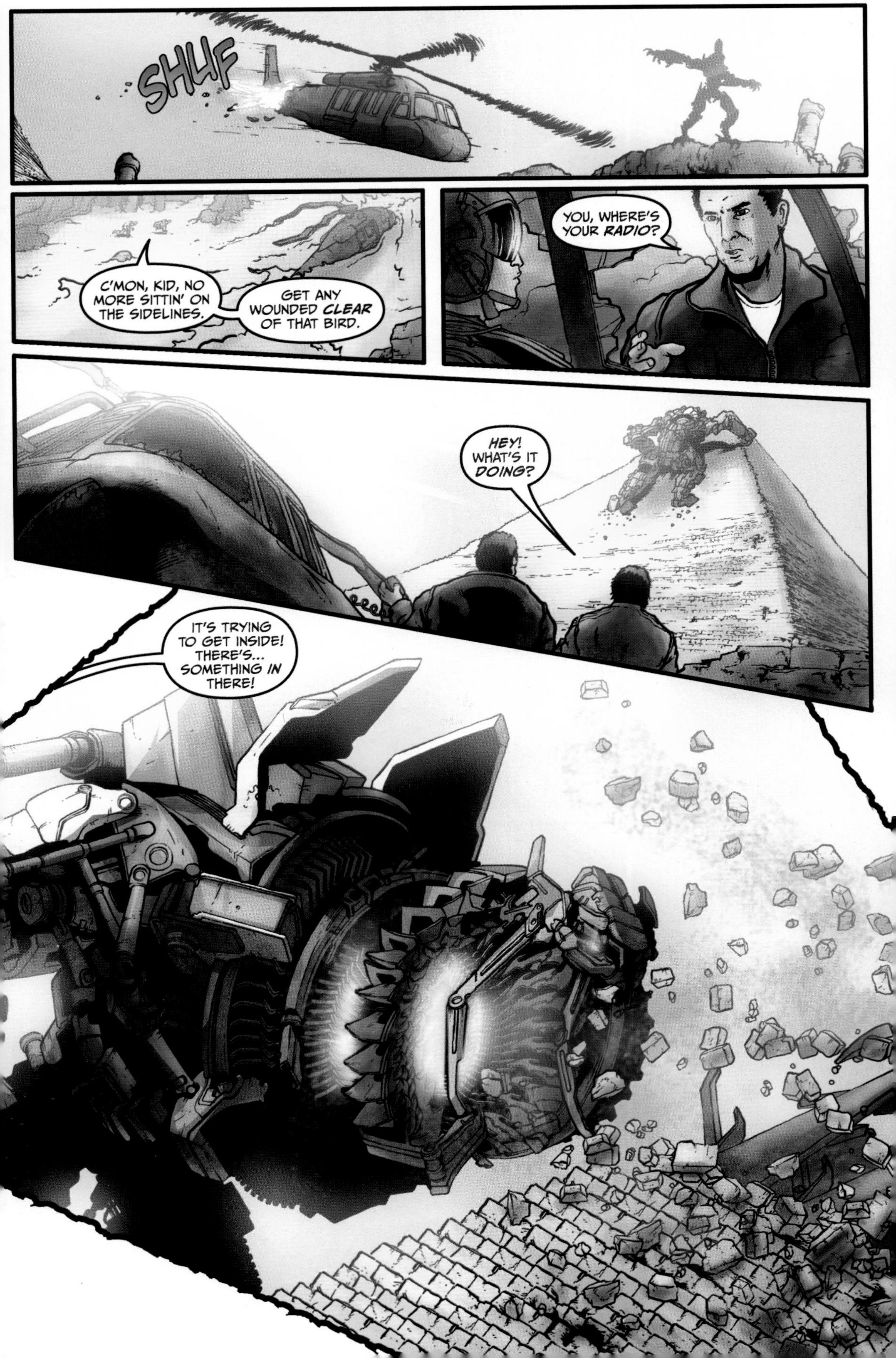
SHUF
C'MON, KID, NO MORE SITTIN' ON THE SIDELINES.
GET ANY WOUNDED CLEAR OF THAT BIRD.
YOU, WHERE'S YOUR RADIO?
HEY! WHAT'S IT DOING?
IT'S TRYING TO GET INSIDE! THERE'S... SOMETHING IN THERE!

"OHMYGOD—THAT'S *IT*. THE MACHINE, THE STAR HARVESTER..."

...THE PYRAMID'S BUILT RIGHT OVER IT!

THE *ENDGAME* IS NIGH!

SWUUUSH

WH—*UUUUH!*

IT'S GOT ME! KID—

I *GOTCHA!* AND IT'S *LEO.* OR SIR.

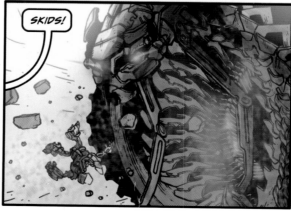

SKIDS!

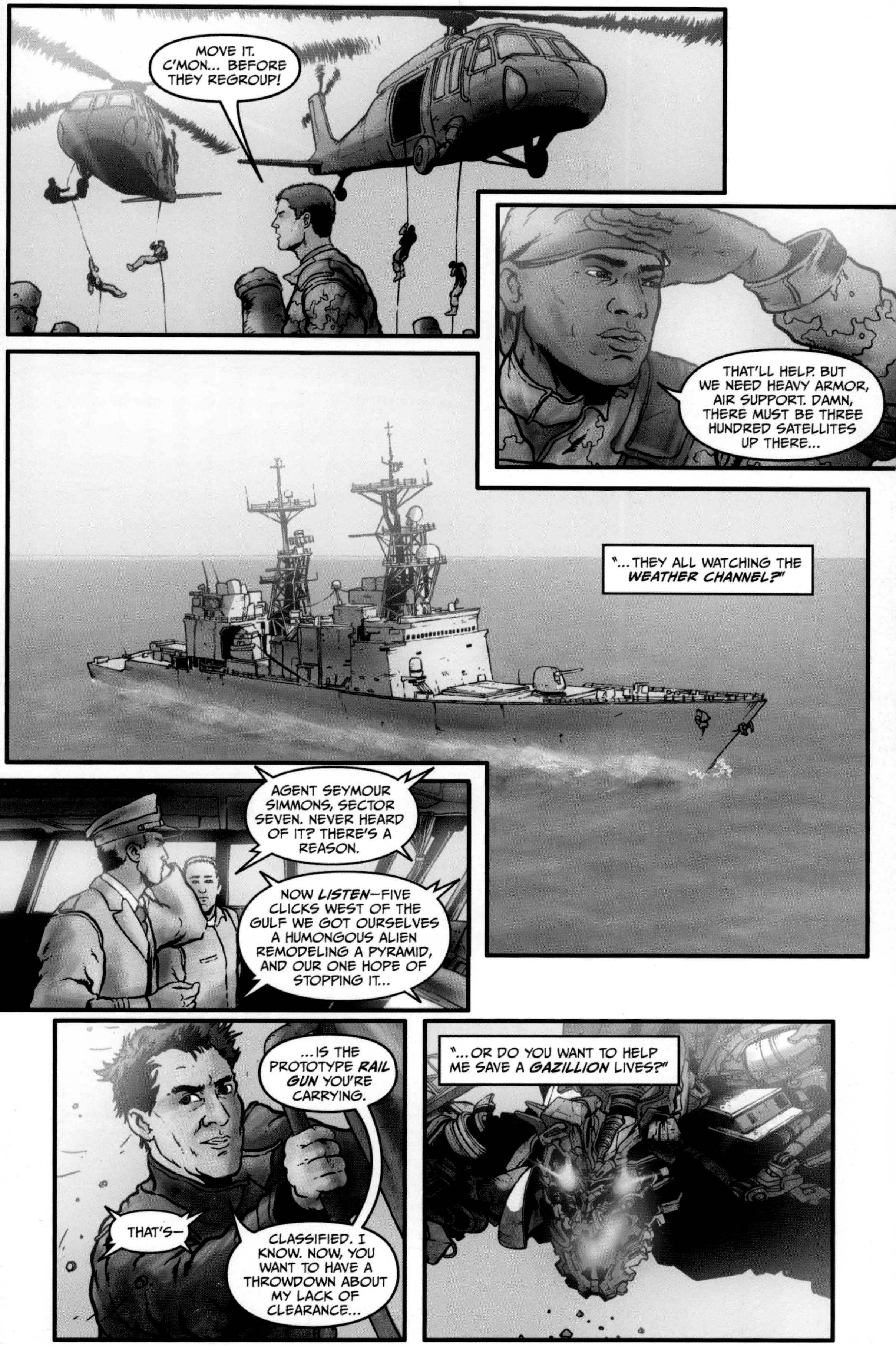
MOVE IT. C'MON... BEFORE THEY REGROUP!
THAT'LL HELP. BUT WE NEED HEAVY ARMOR, AIR SUPPORT. DAMN, THERE MUST BE THREE HUNDRED SATELLITES UP THERE...
"...THEY ALL WATCHING THE WEATHER CHANNEL?"
AGENT SEYMOUR SIMMONS, SECTOR SEVEN. NEVER HEARD OF IT? THERE'S A REASON.
NOW LISTEN—FIVE CLICKS WEST OF THE GULF WE GOT OURSELVES A HUMONGOUS ALIEN REMODELING A PYRAMID, AND OUR ONE HOPE OF STOPPING IT...
...IS THE PROTOTYPE RAIL GUN YOU'RE CARRYING.
THAT'S—
CLASSIFIED. I KNOW. NOW, YOU WANT TO HAVE A THROWDOWN ABOUT MY LACK OF CLEARANCE...
"...OR DO YOU WANT TO HELP ME SAVE A GAZILLION LIVES?"

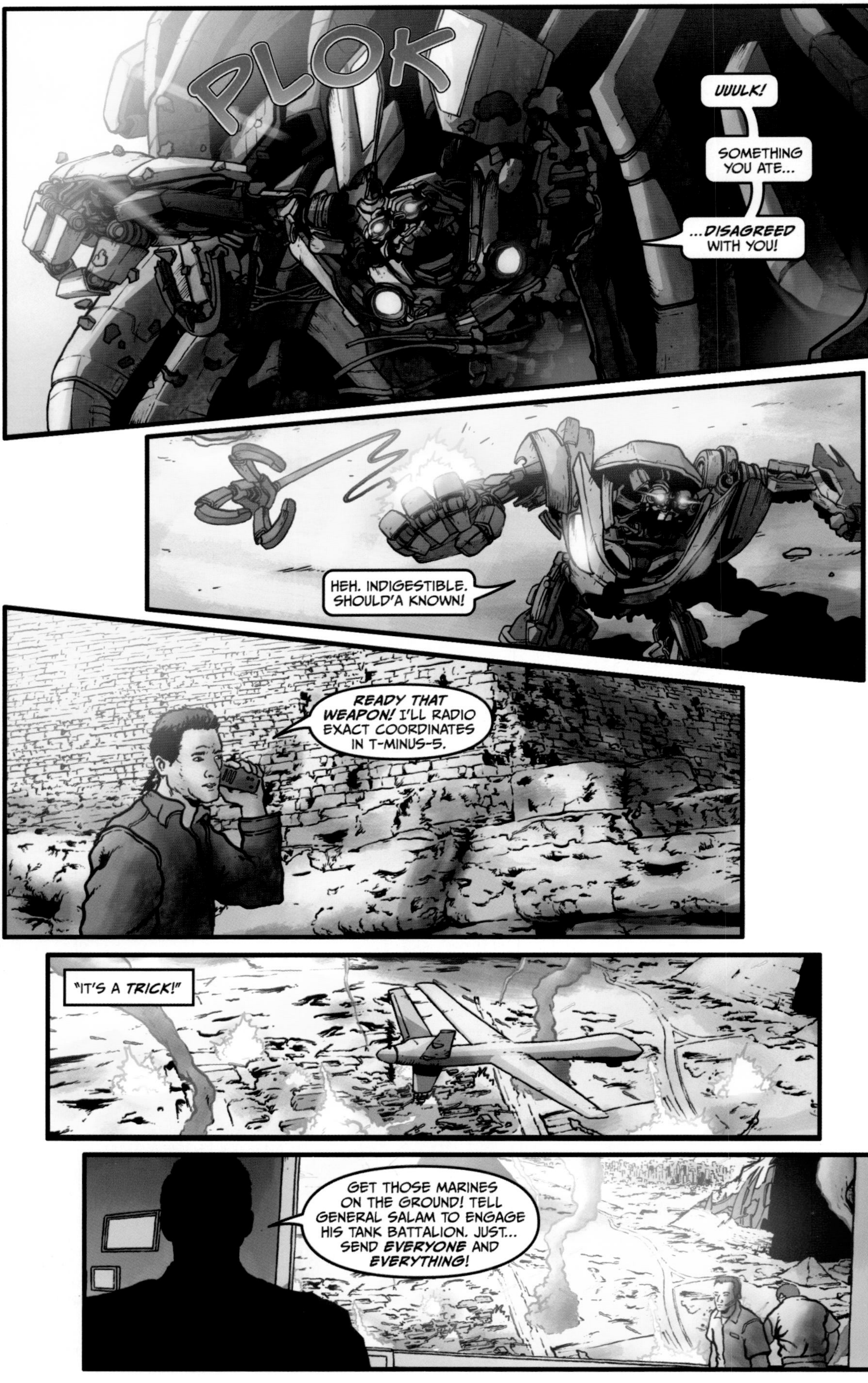

PLOK
UUULK!
SOMETHING YOU ATE...
...DISAGREED WITH YOU!
HEH. INDIGESTIBLE. SHOULD'A KNOWN!
READY THAT WEAPON! I'LL RADIO EXACT COORDINATES IN T-MINUS-5.
"IT'S A TRICK!"
GET THOSE MARINES ON THE GROUND! TELL GENERAL SALAM TO ENGAGE HIS TANK BATTALION. JUST... SEND EVERYONE AND EVERYTHING!

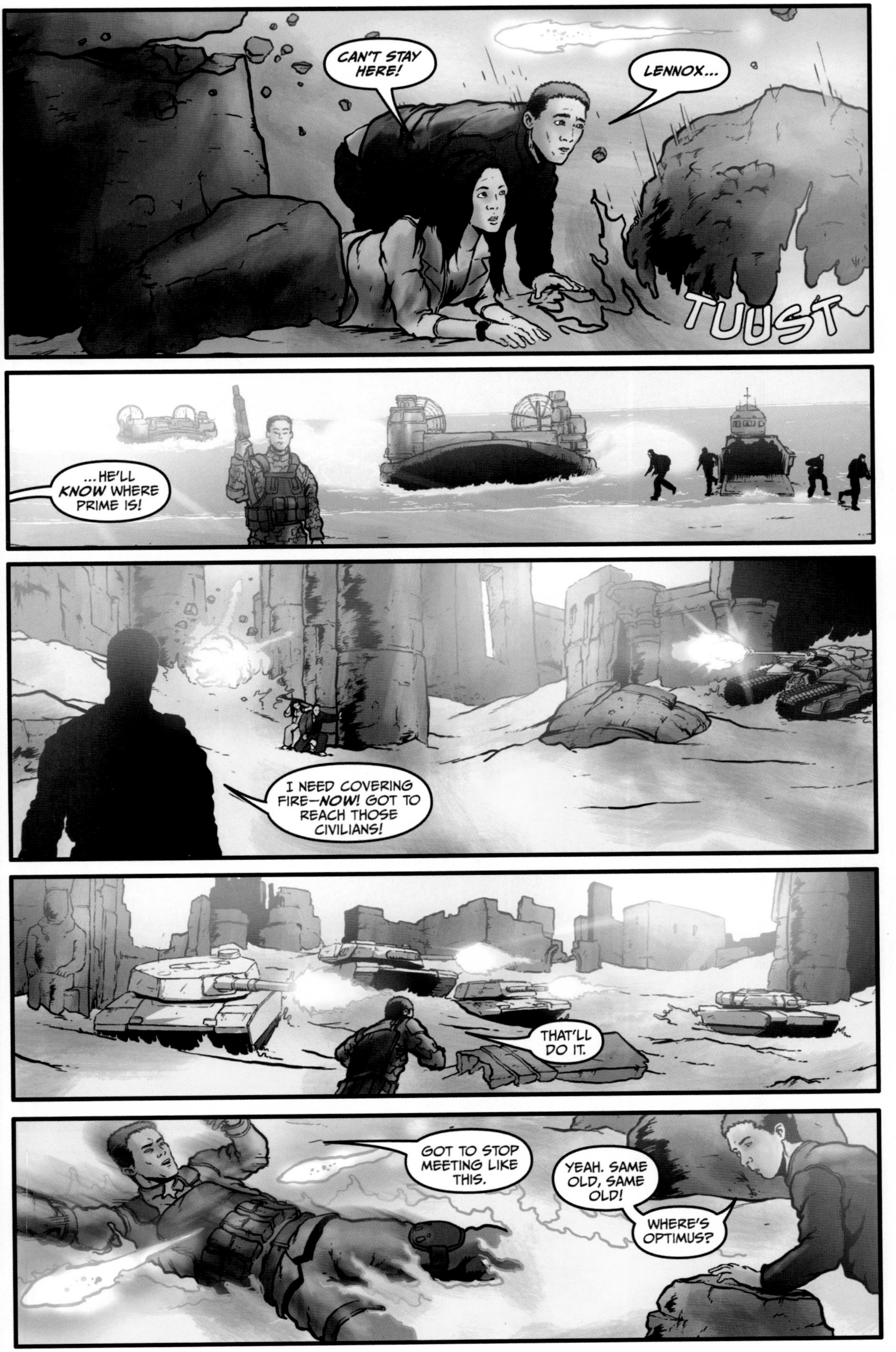
CAN'T STAY HERE!
LENNOX...
TUUST
...HE'LL KNOW WHERE PRIME IS!
I NEED COVERING FIRE—NOW! GOT TO REACH THOSE CIVILIANS!
THAT'LL DO IT.
GOT TO STOP MEETING LIKE THIS.
YEAH. SAME OLD, SAME OLD!
WHERE'S OPTIMUS?

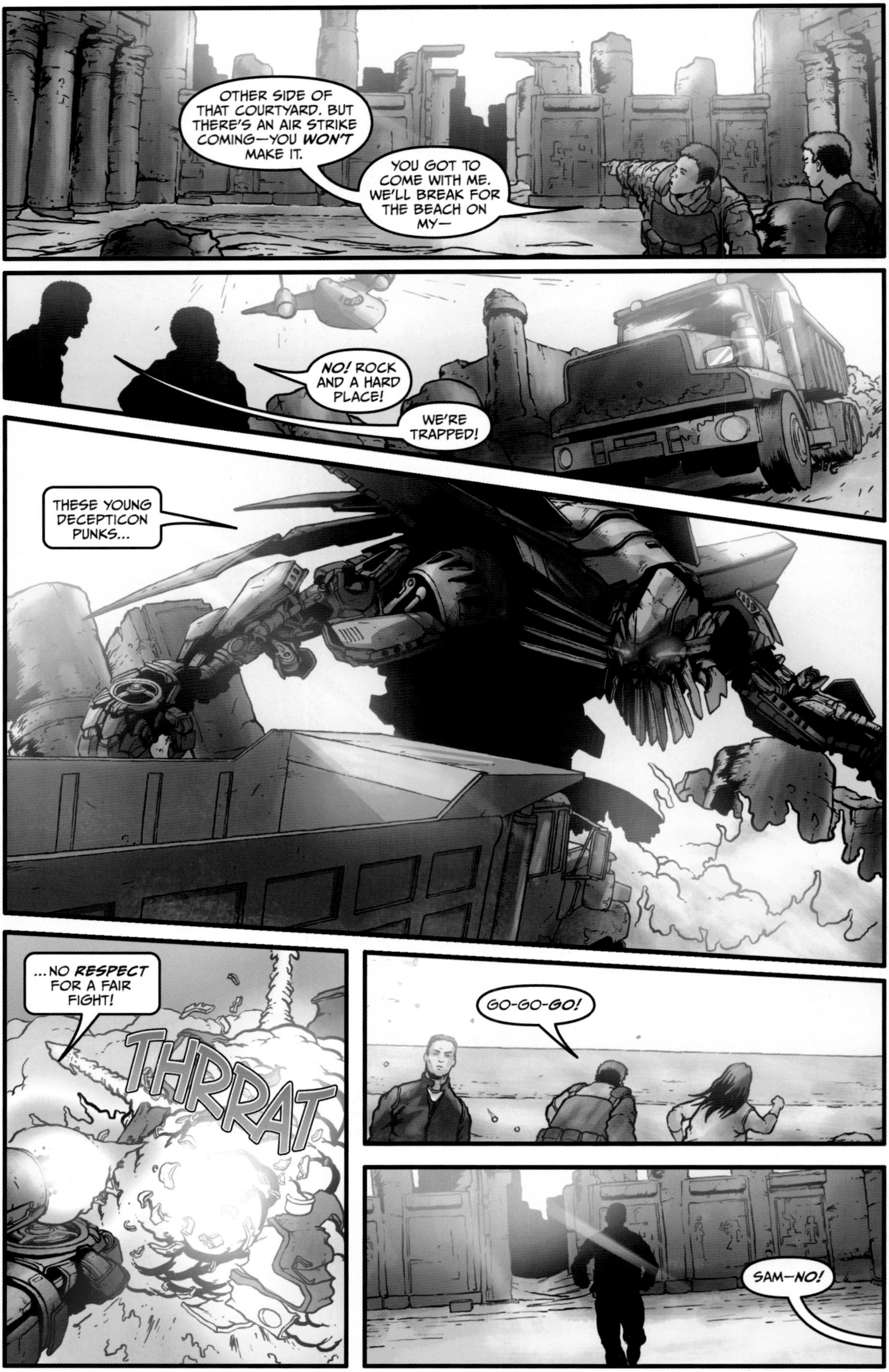
OTHER SIDE OF THAT COURTYARD. BUT THERE'S AN AIR STRIKE COMING—YOU WON'T MAKE IT.
YOU GOT TO COME WITH ME. WE'LL BREAK FOR THE BEACH ON MY—
NO! ROCK AND A HARD PLACE!
WE'RE TRAPPED!
THESE YOUNG DECEPTICON PUNKS...
...NO RESPECT FOR A FAIR FIGHT!
THRRAT
GO-GO-GO!
SAM—NO!

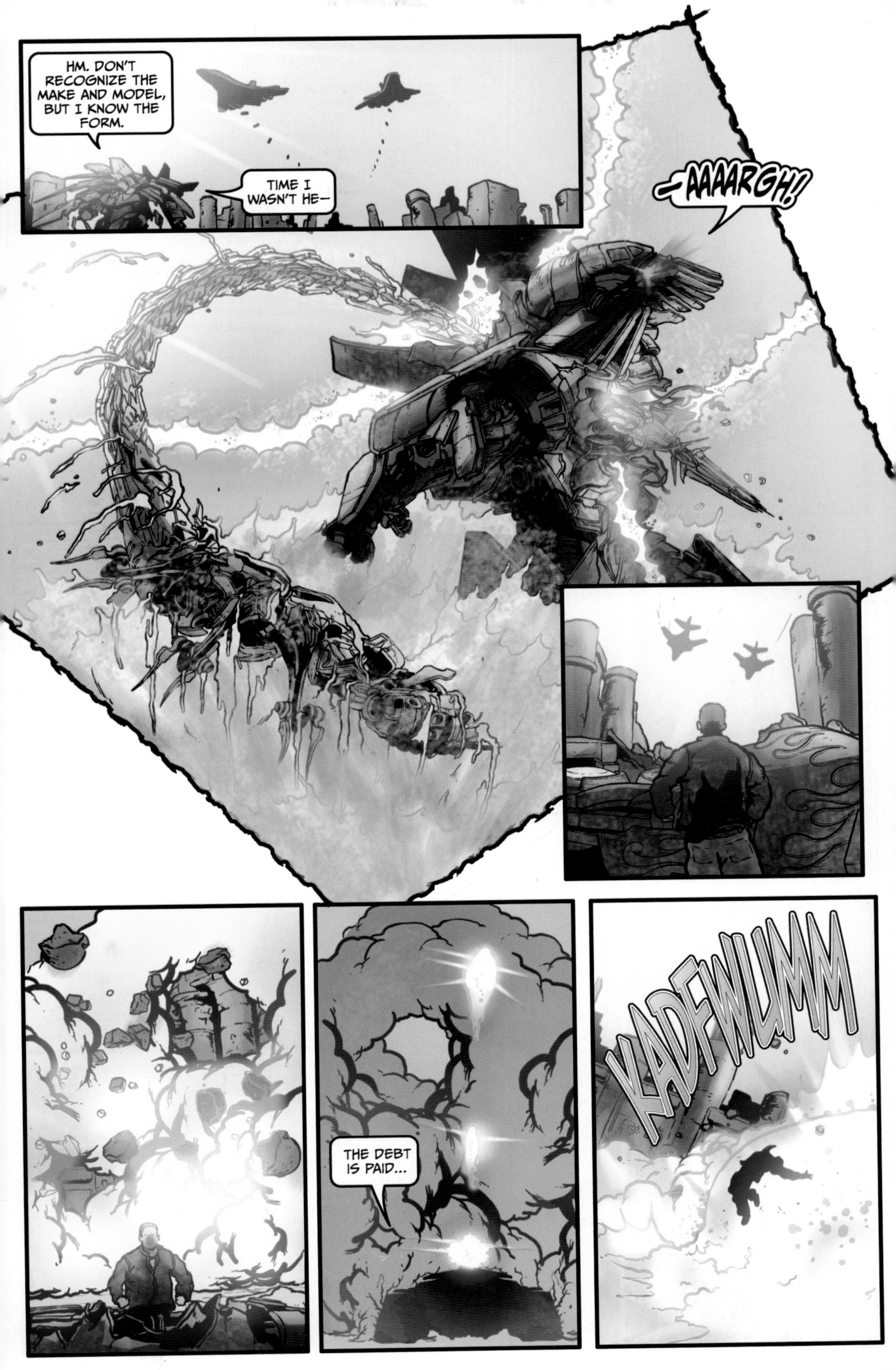
HM. DON'T RECOGNIZE THE MAKE AND MODEL, BUT I KNOW THE FORM.
TIME I WASN'T HE—
—AAAARGH!
THE DEBT IS PAID...
KADFWUMM

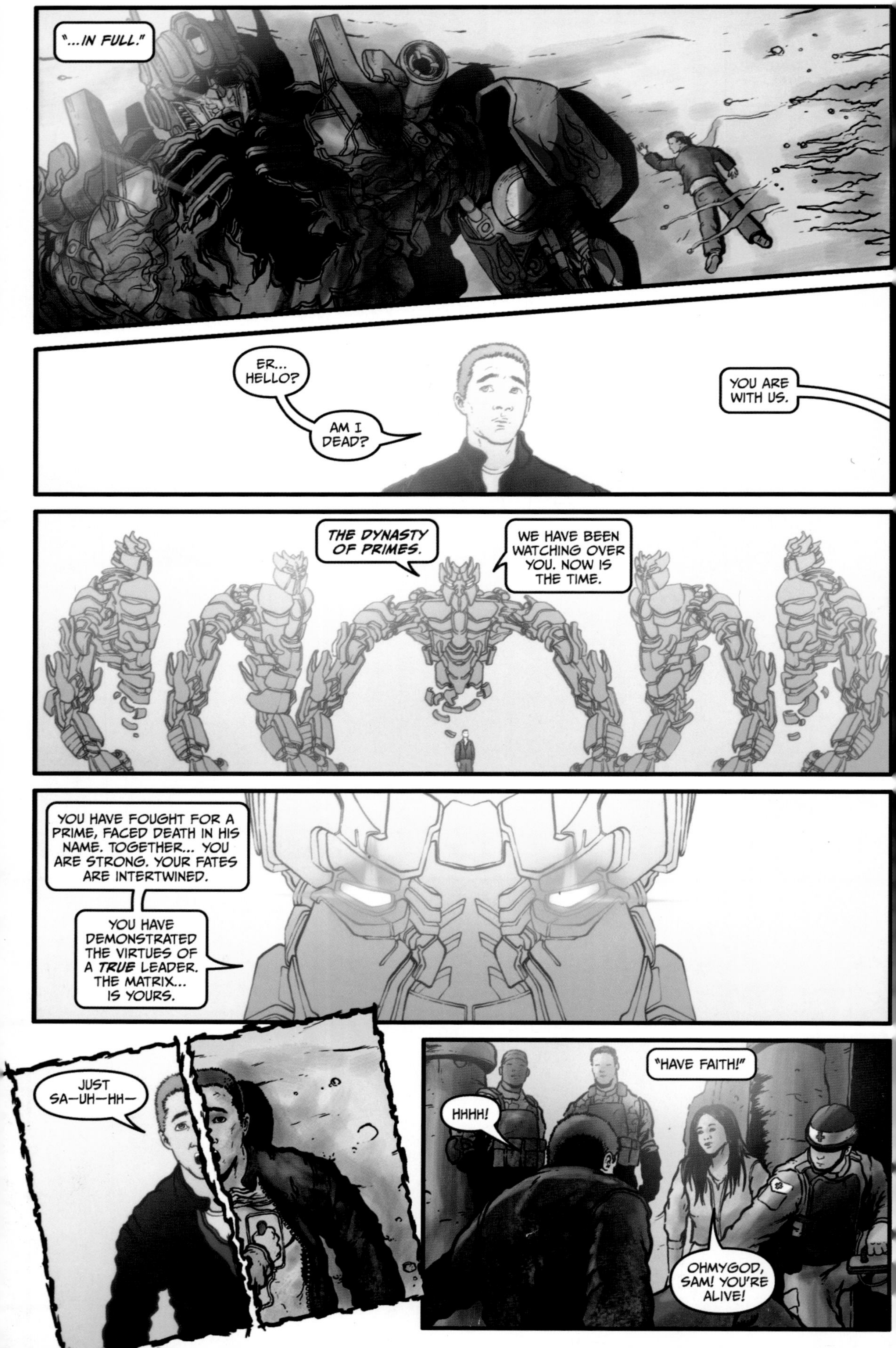
"...IN FULL."
ER... HELLO?
AM I DEAD?
YOU ARE WITH US.
THE DYNASTY OF PRIMES.
WE HAVE BEEN WATCHING OVER YOU. NOW IS THE TIME.
YOU HAVE FOUGHT FOR A PRIME, FACED DEATH IN HIS NAME. TOGETHER... YOU ARE STRONG. YOUR FATES ARE INTERTWINED.
YOU HAVE DEMONSTRATED THE VIRTUES OF A TRUE LEADER. THE MATRIX... IS YOURS.
JUST SA—UH—HH—
"HAVE FAITH!"
HHHH!
OHMYGOD, SAM! YOU'RE ALIVE!

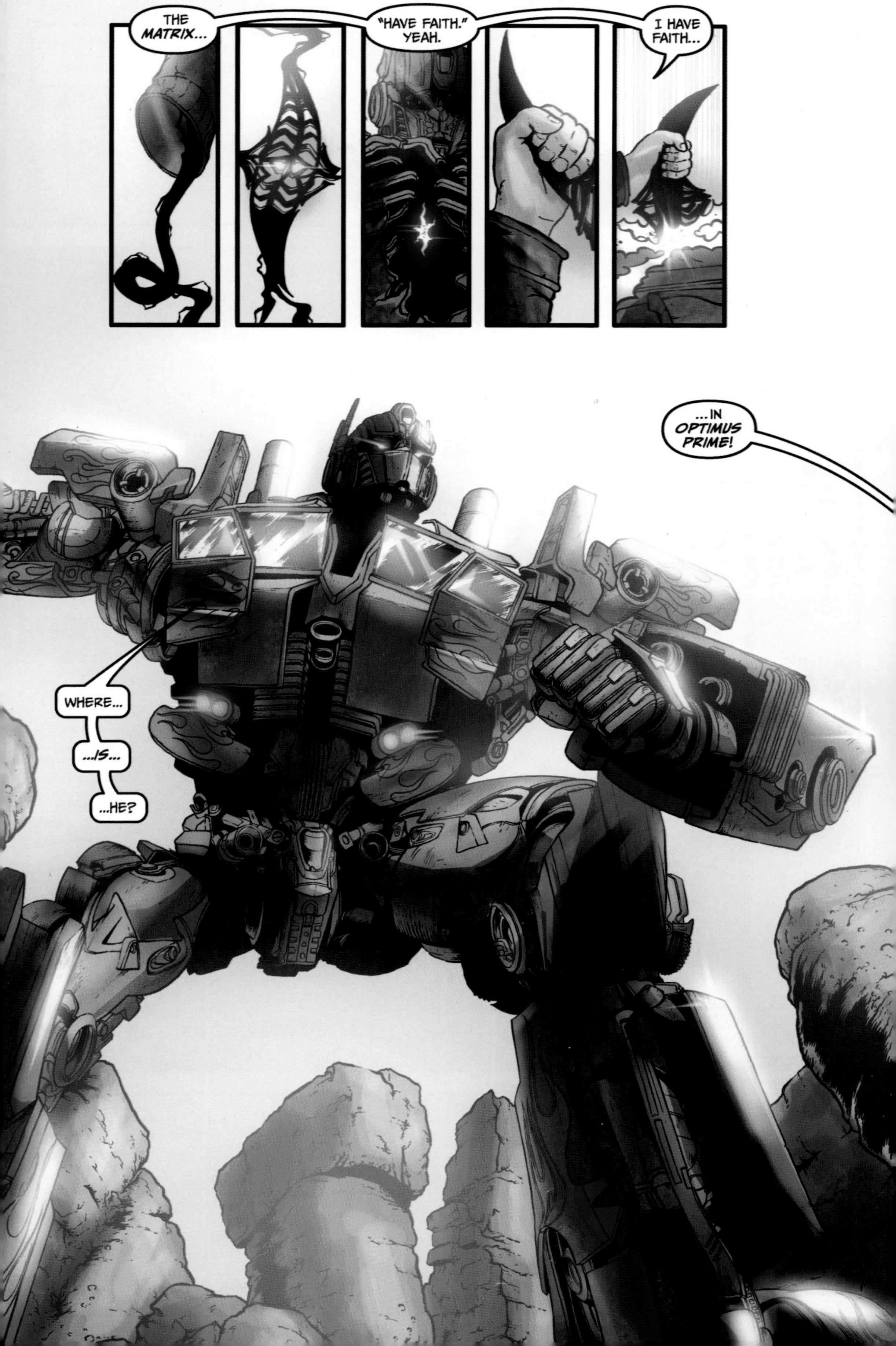
THE MATRIX...
"HAVE FAITH." YEAH.
I HAVE FAITH...
...IN OPTIMUS PRIME!
WHERE...
...IS...
...HE?

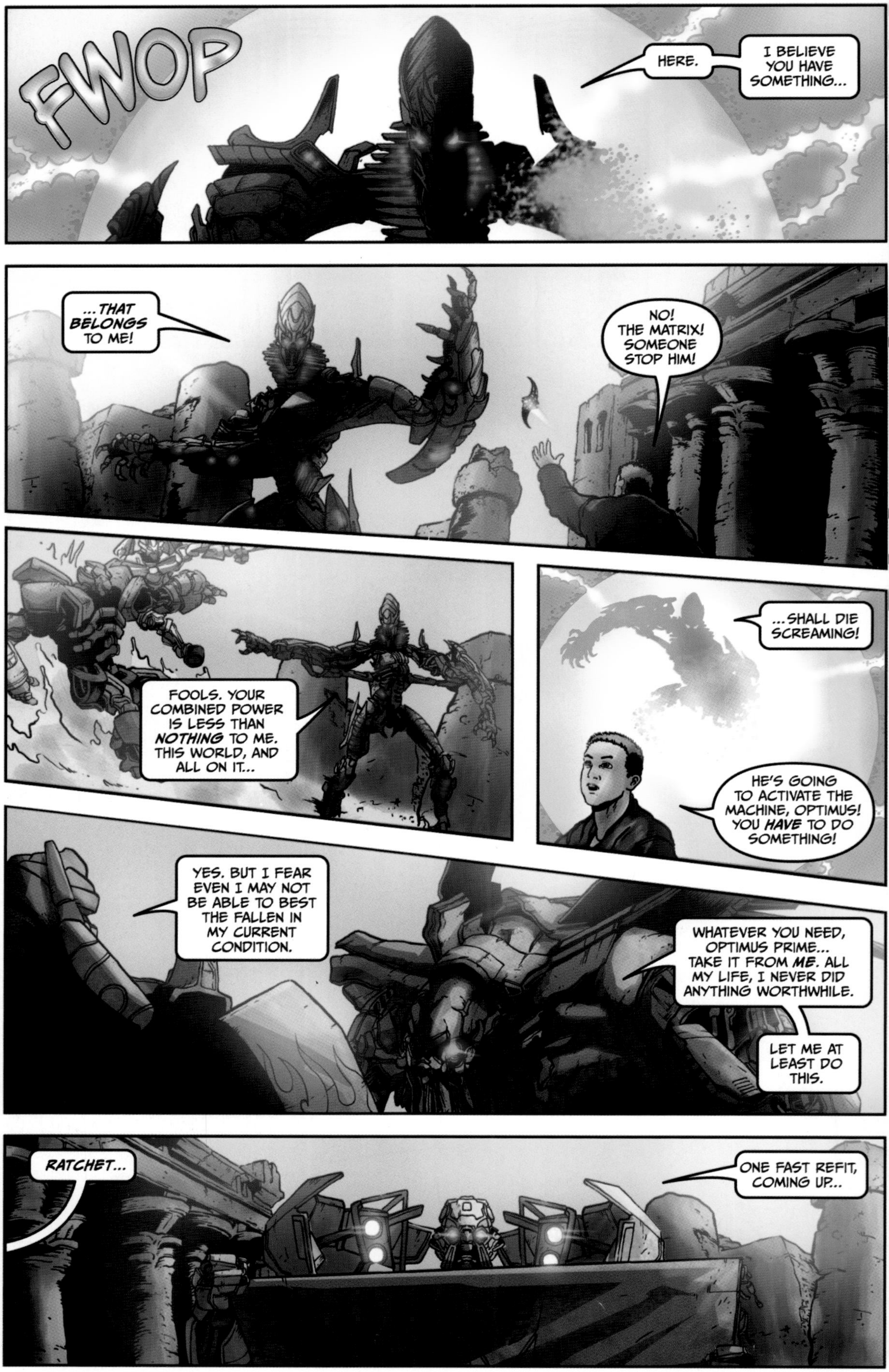
FWOP
HERE.
I BELIEVE YOU HAVE SOMETHING...
...THAT BELONGS TO ME!
NO! THE MATRIX! SOMEONE STOP HIM!
FOOLS. YOUR COMBINED POWER IS LESS THAN NOTHING TO ME. THIS WORLD, AND ALL ON IT...
...SHALL DIE SCREAMING!
HE'S GOING TO ACTIVATE THE MACHINE, OPTIMUS! YOU HAVE TO DO SOMETHING!
YES. BUT I FEAR EVEN I MAY NOT BE ABLE TO BEST THE FALLEN IN MY CURRENT CONDITION.
WHATEVER YOU NEED, OPTIMUS PRIME... TAKE IT FROM ME. ALL MY LIFE, I NEVER DID ANYTHING WORTHWHILE.
LET ME AT LEAST DO THIS.
RATCHET...
ONE FAST REFIT, COMING UP...

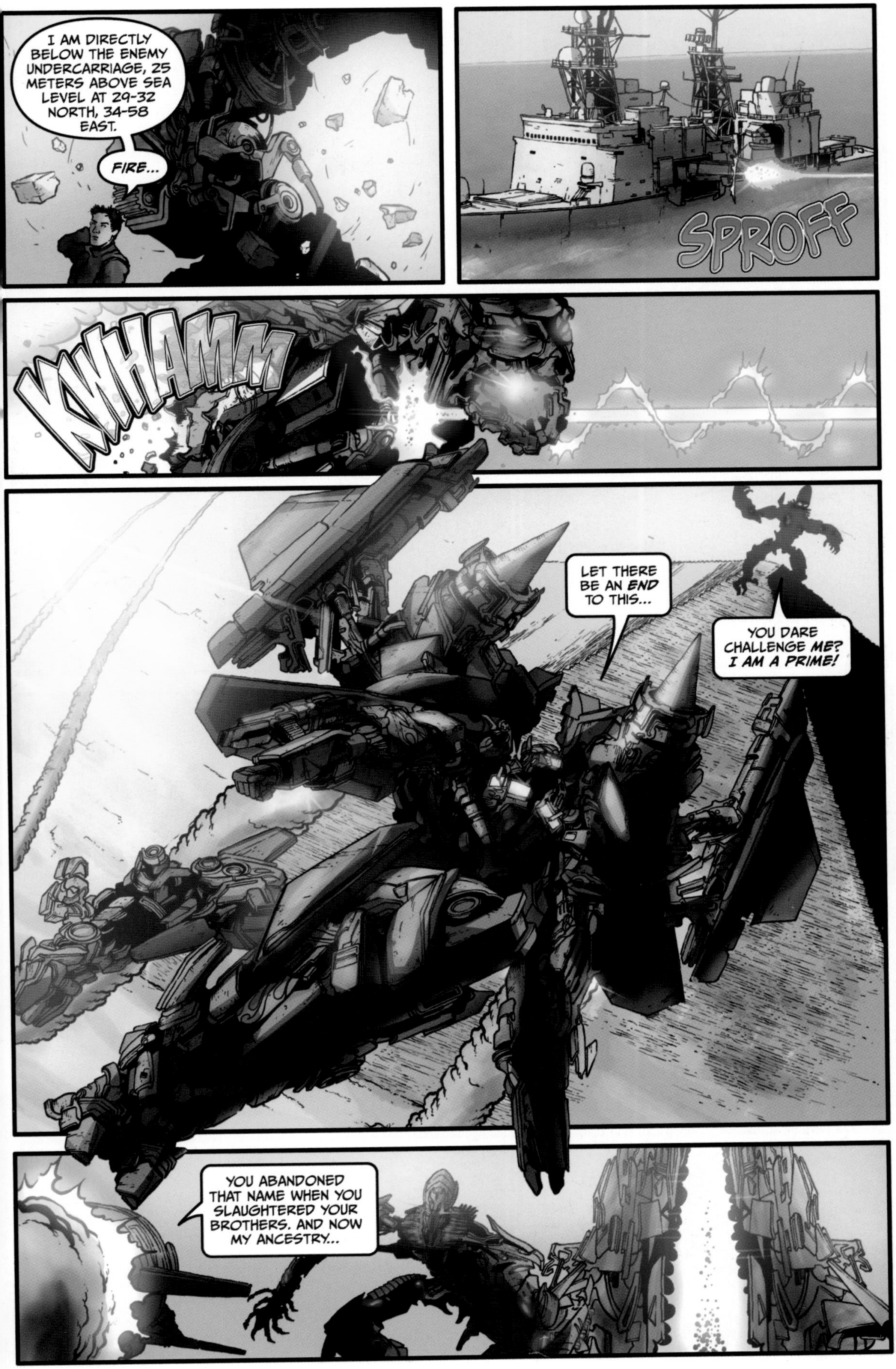
I AM DIRECTLY BELOW THE ENEMY UNDERCARRIAGE, 25 METERS ABOVE SEA LEVEL AT 29-32 NORTH, 34-58 EAST.
FIRE...
SPROFF
KWHAMM
LET THERE BE AN END TO THIS...
YOU DARE CHALLENGE ME? I AM A PRIME!
YOU ABANDONED THAT NAME WHEN YOU SLAUGHTERED YOUR BROTHERS. AND NOW MY ANCESTRY...

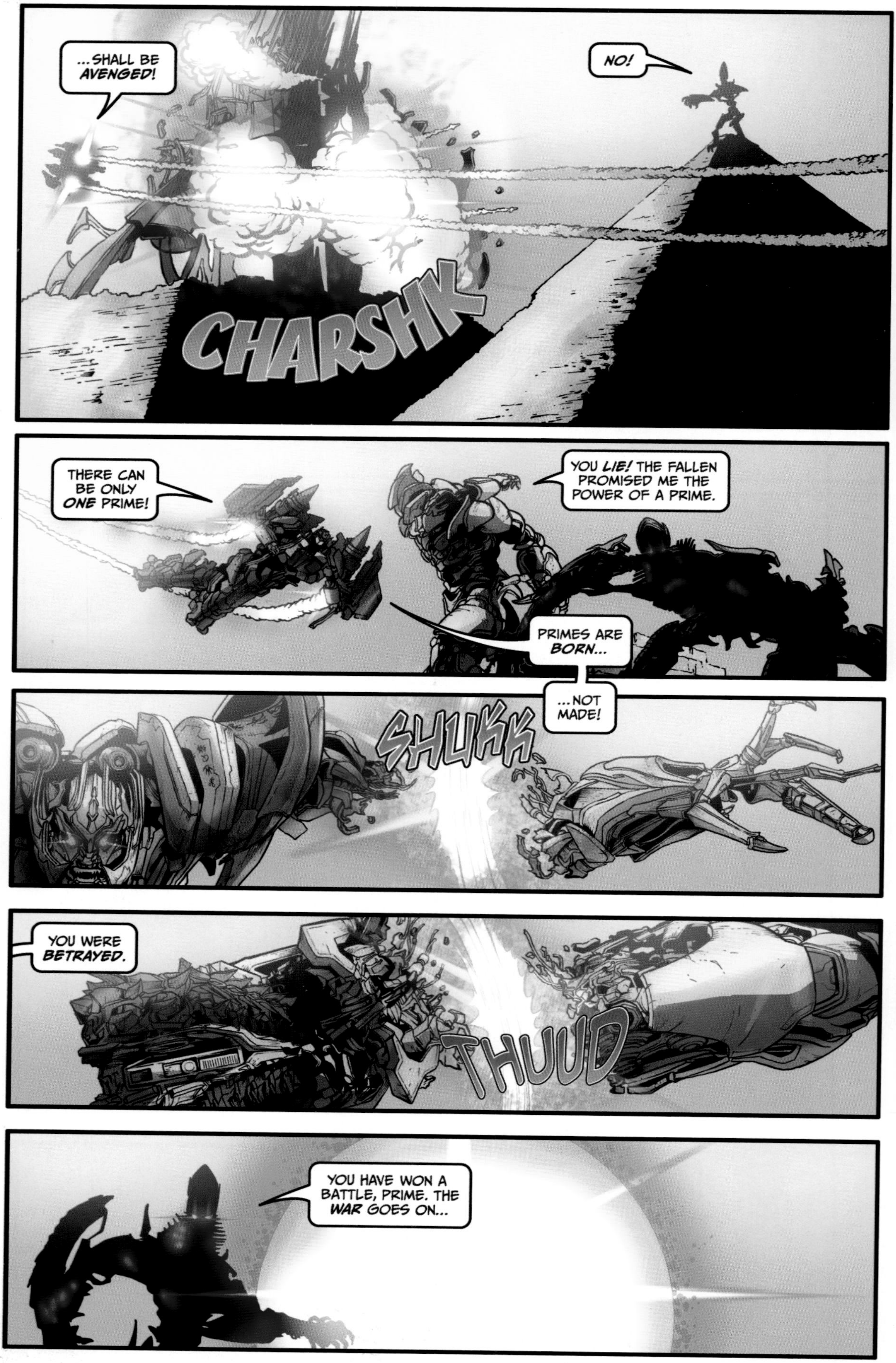
...SHALL BE AVENGED!
NO!
CHARSHK
THERE CAN BE ONLY ONE PRIME!
YOU LIE! THE FALLEN PROMISED ME THE POWER OF A PRIME.
PRIMES ARE BORN...
...NOT MADE!
SHUKK
YOU WERE BETRAYED.
THUUD
YOU HAVE WON A BATTLE, PRIME. THE WAR GOES ON...

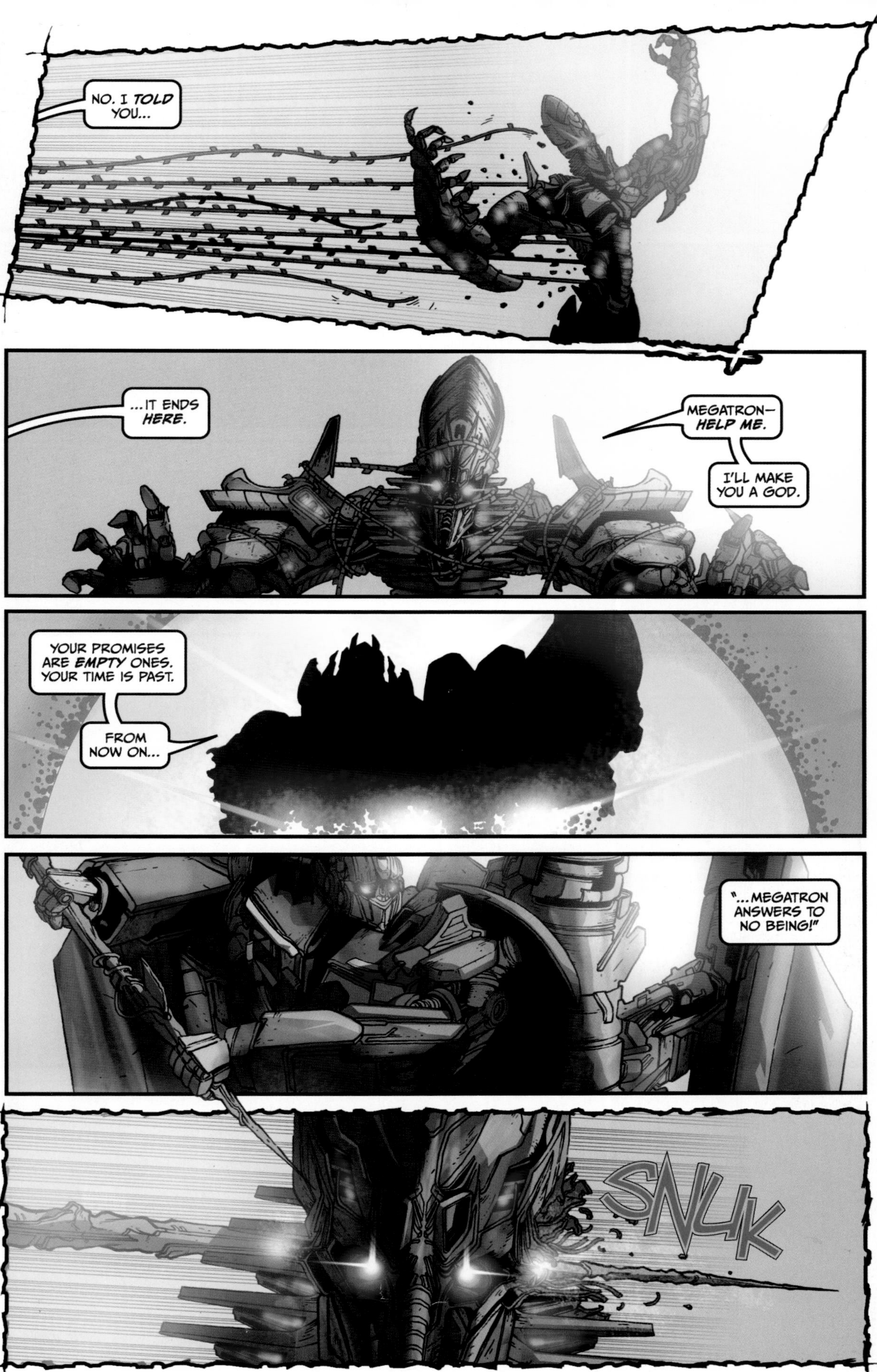
NO. I TOLD YOU...
...IT ENDS HERE.
MEGATRON— HELP ME.
I'LL MAKE YOU A GOD.
YOUR PROMISES ARE EMPTY ONES. YOUR TIME IS PAST.
FROM NOW ON...
"...MEGATRON ANSWERS TO NO BEING!"
SNUK

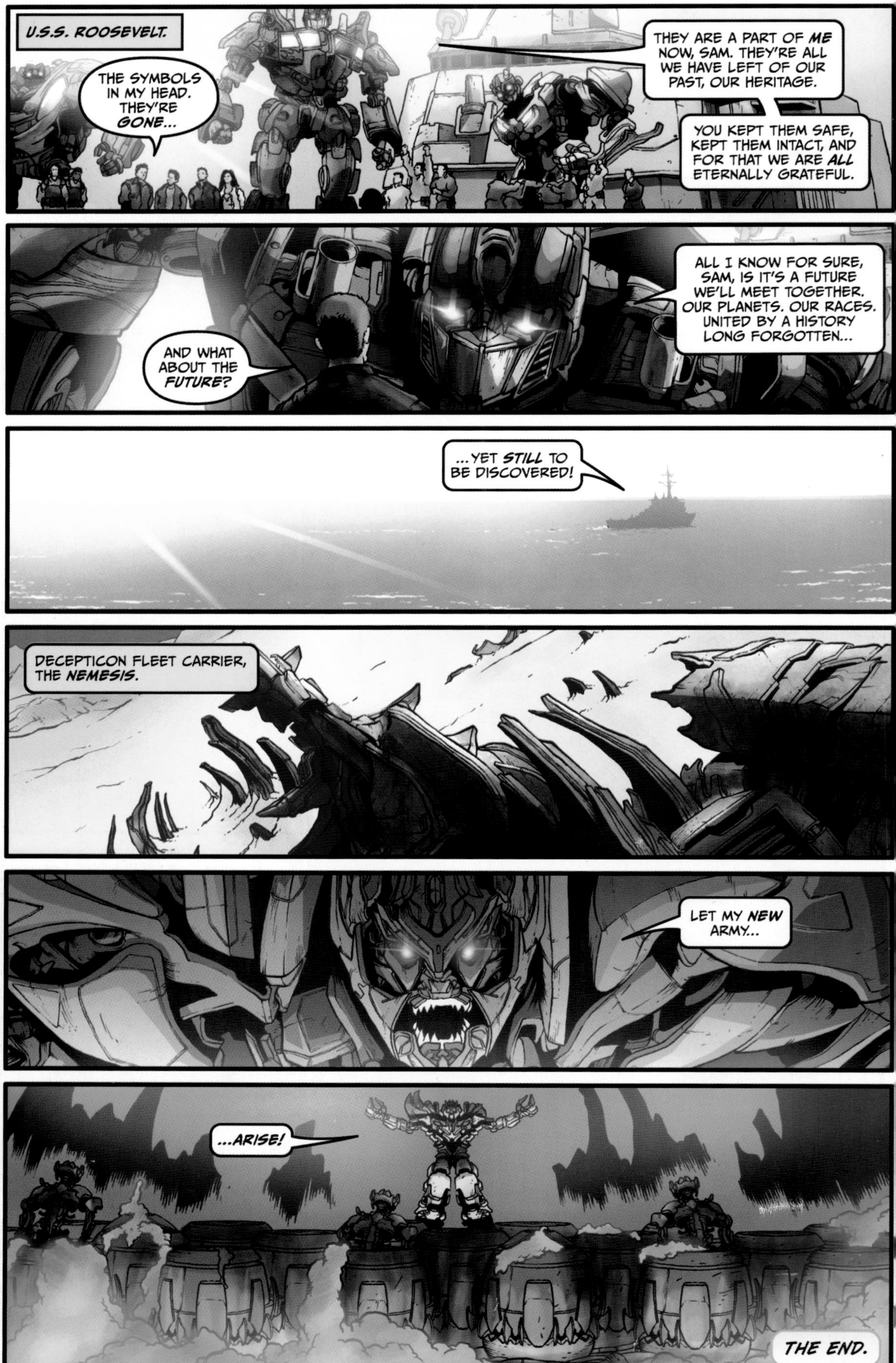
U.S.S. ROOSEVELT.
THE SYMBOLS IN MY HEAD. THEY'RE GONE...
THEY ARE A PART OF ME NOW, SAM. THEY'RE ALL WE HAVE LEFT OF OUR PAST, OUR HERITAGE.
YOU KEPT THEM SAFE, KEPT THEM INTACT, AND FOR THAT WE ARE ALL ETERNALLY GRATEFUL.
AND WHAT ABOUT THE FUTURE?
ALL I KNOW FOR SURE, SAM, IS IT'S A FUTURE WE'LL MEET TOGETHER. OUR PLANETS. OUR RACES. UNITED BY A HISTORY LONG FORGOTTEN...
...YET STILL TO BE DISCOVERED!
DECEPTICON FLEET CARRIER, THE NEMESIS.
LET MY NEW ARMY...
...ARISE!
THE END.